This Little Tiger book belongs to:

_____

_____

_____

For Bob and Sue
~ N. W.

LITTLE TIGER PRESS LTD,
an imprint of the Little Tiger Group
1 The Coda Centre, 189 Munster Road, London SW6 6AW
www.littletiger.co.uk

First published in Great Britain 2005
This edition published 2017

Printed in China
LTP/1800/1895/0717

2 4 6 8 10 9 7 5 3 1

The BIGGEST BADDEST WOLF

by Nick Ward

LITTLE TIGER
LONDON

"I am the GREATEST!"

howled Harum Scarum, admiring himself
in the mirror as he brushed his fangs.
"I am the biggest, baddest, hairiest,
scariest wolf in the city!"

FUR GEL

SHAMPOO
for extra
coarse hair

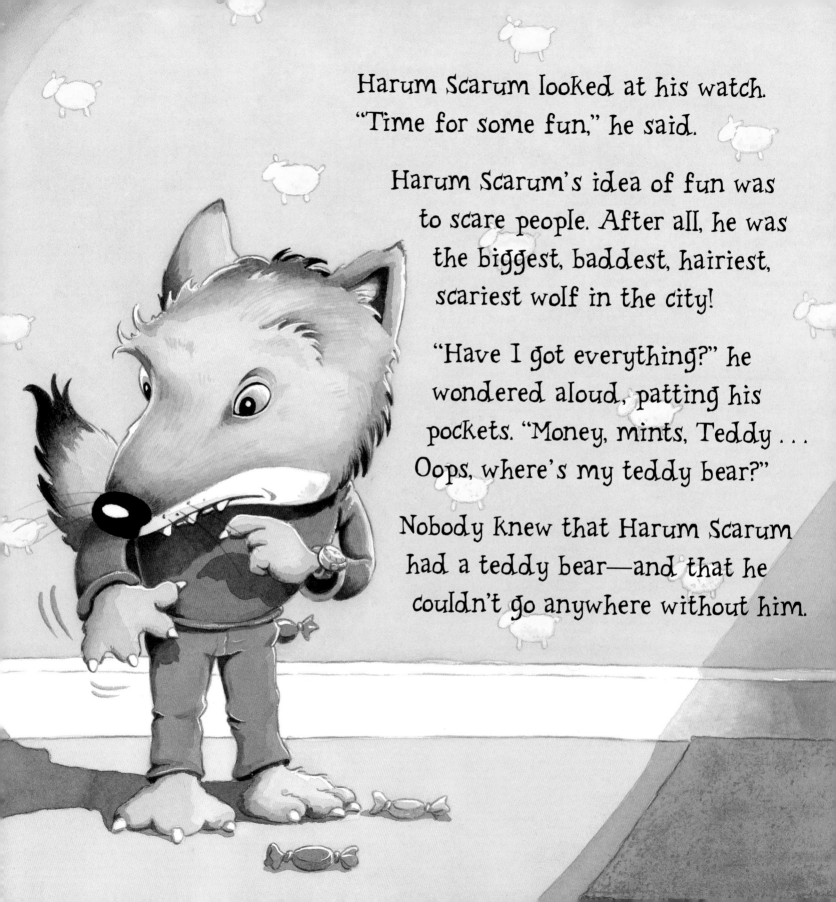

Harum Scarum looked at his watch. "Time for some fun," he said.

Harum Scarum's idea of fun was to scare people. After all, he was the biggest, baddest, hairiest, scariest wolf in the city!

"Have I got everything?" he wondered aloud, patting his pockets. "Money, mints, Teddy . . . Oops, where's my teddy bear?"

Nobody knew that Harum Scarum had a teddy bear—and that he couldn't go anywhere without him.

"Ah! There you are!"
he cried, giving Teddy
a big, wet, wolfy kiss.

He put Teddy in his
back pocket and happily
stepped out for the day.

First stop was the park, where Harum Scarum had some fun scaring all the little children playing on the swings.

"Run, little children, run, or I'll eat you up!"

he howled.

"Eeek!" they screamed and ran away.

"I am the biggest, baddest, hairiest, scariest wolf in the city!" he called after them.

Harum Scarum moved on to the bus stop,
where a group of old people were waiting.

"Run, old people, run,
or I'll eat you up!"

he howled.

"Eeek!" they screamed,
and tottered all the way home.

"I am the biggest, baddest, hairiest, scariest
wolf in the city!" he called after them.

For the rest of the day, Harum Scarum worked very hard at scaring anyone he could.

He **startled** a skateboarder . . . .

He **petrified** a builder . . . .

And he made a street juggler jump.

"Now this is what I call fun!" he cried.

By the time he got home, he was so tired he decided to go straight to bed.

And that's when he discovered ... he'd lost his teddy bear!

"Oh no!" he said, frantically searching his room. He looked here and there ... but he couldn't find Teddy anywhere.

Harum Scarum crawled sadly into bed.
He tossed and turned, but he couldn't get
to sleep without his teddy bear to cuddle.

The next morning Harum Scarum was a nervous wreck.
"I must find my teddy bear," he wailed, and hurried
outside without even brushing his fangs.

He paced the streets.

He searched in every alley.

He looked high . . .

and low . . .

But Teddy was nowhere to be seen.

Finally Harum Scarum arrived at the bus stop.
"Excuse me, have you seen a teddy bear?"
he asked the old people.

But as soon as they saw him, they tottered off home shouting, "Help, it's the biggest, baddest, hairiest, scariest wolf in the city!"

Harum Scarum went to the park. "Excuse me . . ."
he began, but the little children all ran away
shouting, "Help, it's the biggest, baddest, hairiest,
scariest wolf in the city!"

Harum Scarum sighed, and a tear rolled down his cheek. But just then he noticed one little boy left playing on his own. And he was playing with . . . Harum Scarum's teddy bear!

"My teddy bear!" gasped Harum Scarum.

"MY teddy bear!" said the little boy.
"Finders Keepers."

"Please give him back,"
Harum Scarum whimpered.
"I'm the biggest, baddest,
hairiest, scariest wolf
in the city."

"You don't look so scary to me," said the little boy.

"Please!" cried Harum Scarum. "I'd do anything to get Teddy back."

"Do you promise to do exactly what you're told from now on?" asked the little boy.

"Of course," he said.

The very next morning, after a good night's sleep, Harum Scarum brushed his fangs and patted his pockets. Whistling happily, he left home and went straight to the park.

"Hurry up," cried the little children. "We're on the swings! Come and push us."

"Coming," called Harum Scarum with a smile. He trotted up to the children . . .

"Run, little children, run, or I'll eat you up!"

"Eeek!" cried the children, rushing away. "You promised . . ."

"Well, what did you expect?" asked
    Harum Scarum, hugging his teddy bear.
"You should NEVER trust the biggest,
    baddest, hairiest, scariest wolf in the city!"